VANISHING VILLAGE

HAZEL TOWNSON

Andersen Press
LONDON

For AUDREY ADAMS,
my editor for twenty-five years, with thanks for
all that boundless patience, wisdom, support
and understanding, and with best wishes for
a long and happy retirement

First published in 2007 by
Andersen Press Limited,
20 Vauxhall Bridge Road, London SW1V 2SA

British Library Cataloguing in Publication Data available

ISBN 978 1 84270 472 1

Typeset by FiSH Books, Enfield, Middx.
Printed and bound in Great Britain by
Bookmarque Ltd., Croydon, Surrey

1

Saturday, 14th July

Either I'm going mad or this house is haunted. All night I've been hearing these moaning noises in the attic. Mum says it's just that old houses talk to themselves, creaking and shifting and sighing; or maybe it's the wind caught in the gap made by the missing roof tiles. But I know otherwise. Anyone as depressed as I am is a perfect prey for all sorts of horrors. Poltergeists, maybe.

Gran always said it was bad luck to move house on a Friday, and I knew she was right when our removal van squelched up that final muddy lane yesterday and I caught the first glimpse of this dump. The garden's a jungle, the paintwork's a faded memory and the front bay window's cracked. And that's before you lift your eyes to the weather-battered roof that even the magpies shun.

For days before we moved here Mum kept boasting about her 'bargain buy', but some crafty crook had obviously seen her coming. If only she'd let Dad look the place over first... but she wanted to do it all herself, to prove she could manage without him.

Dad's new flat is a much sounder proposition; a bit cramped, but at least he's managed to stay in civilised Manchester. I can't wait for my next monthly weekend visit, despite the limited space – though considering my state of mind, who's to say that won't be haunted, too? I read somewhere that an uneasy mind carries its own ghosts around with it.

Mum and I spent the whole of yesterday heaving furniture and unpacking boxes, seeing nobody except the removal men. But this morning the first local yokel showed up. I was struggling out to the dustbin with armfuls of packaging and empty boxes when this girl appeared.

'You the new neighbours, then?' she

asked, propping herself and her bike against our gate. I felt like saying, 'No; I'm the dustman,' but I didn't want to encourage some sarky reply so I kept quiet.

She was a tall, skinny creature about my age, dressed in faded green shorts and orange T-shirt, with rusty hair blown all over the place and cheeky brown eyes; persistent, too.

'My name's Ellie, short for Eloise – Eloise Bradman; what's yours?'

Eloise? I sneered to myself. What sort of name was that to give to a country bumpkin? Didn't really blend in with all this mud and bramble.

'Well, come on, your turn,' the bumpkin insisted.

Surely she could see I wasn't in the mood? I made a big, fierce production of stamping the air out of cardboard boxes. But just then Mum appeared, bearing more rubbish. As usual she'd had her ears pricked up; never misses a trick.

'His name's biblical,' she announced. 'New Testament, have a guess.'

'Job? Jeremiah?' giggled Bumpkin. 'Oh

no, they're Old Testament. Judas, then?'

I scowled a death-beam at Mum.

'Matthew,' Mum corrected. 'Matthew Padstow. Matt to his friends, and I'm his mum, Valerie. We're both pleased to meet you,' she added pointedly, glaring back at me. 'Good timing, Ellie, you can fill us in on the local lore. Matt reckons this house is haunted.'

'Believe in ghosts, do you?' Ellie's eyes widened mischievously.

'Keep an open mind,' said Mum. 'Always willing to hear all sides of a story.'

It was a stupid conversation and I was furious with Mum. I banged down the dustbin lid and started to walk away.

Ellie took a deep breath. 'Well,' she said, shifting along to lean eagerly over our crumbling wall, 'as you must know, this place has been empty for ages, so myths do tend to form. People get suspicious of long-time-empty houses and when they're suspicious they start rumours which grow into myths.'

'What sort of myths?' asked Mum. 'Go on; I'm intrigued.'

Just then I happened to be chasing some

stray bits of litter that had blown towards the gate so I couldn't help overhearing. This Ellie, plainly determined to make the most of her captive audience – there couldn't be many of those out here in the sticks – piled on the drama. 'Oh, it's a weird tale from years ago, well before my time. Apparently the last lot of tenants, mum, dad and daughter, took in this strange woman lodger who turned up unexpectedly, told them a sob story about being homeless and pregnant, and persuaded them to let her stay. Nobody knows what really went on, but the family suddenly disappeared, leaving all their belongings behind. They never got in touch again or made any effort to claim their stuff. Then the daughter was found drowned in the river and the lodger was arrested – supposed to have murdered her, and quite likely the missing parents as well, though as far as I know, no trace of them was ever found.

'Eventually, the new owner cleared the place, gave all their stuff to charity and tried in vain to sell the house. Then he tried to let it, but couldn't find any takers. Not surprising really. Nobody's lived here since.'

'That's quite a story,' said Mum, 'but you can't leave us in suspense. What happened to the woman lodger? Was she convicted? And what about her baby?'

Ellie shrugged. 'There are lots of different versions. You know how it is; tales get embroidered; somebody twists things round or a bit gets added on every time. Some say she did end up in prison, had her baby there, might even have died there. But then again, there are others who reckon she got off scot-free, or went to jail and escaped. They say she still turns up from time to time, usually at night, skulking about the place in search of new victims. I don't know whether I should tell you this, but late-night passers-by sometimes claim to have heard strange moaning noises coming from your upstairs.'

'You don't say!' grinned Mum, enjoying herself hugely. In fact, I could see plots already forming, Mum being Valerie Padstow, struggling romantic novelist. (Not first-rate literature, but hopefully sufficient now to scrape us a living.)

'So we may well be haunted after all?' Mum spoke as if this were the house's crowning glory. As for me, my depression deepened; I'd been right all along.

'Yeah, we're all haunted here,' agreed Ellie. 'Spelswick the Ghost Village, that's what we've become. No proper facilities, no public transport, nothing to do, nowhere to go, nobody to care. If you don't believe me, ask anyone.'

'I expect we'll find out for ourselves,' smiled Mum. 'But it doesn't seem to be doing you any harm. I'm sure there are plenty of compensations.'

I didn't like the way those two were getting on. For the only redeeming feature of this house had to be its isolation, offering a chance for me to nurse my wounds in private, and I'd been planning on keeping it that way. But now it seemed author Valerie had other ideas.

'Tell you what, why don't you come in and look round?' she invited Ellie. 'See if you can pick up any ghostly vibes.'

'It's not safe for visitors yet,' I snarled.

Well, there was stuff lying about all over the place, just waiting for someone to fall over it and break a limb.

'Oh, don't mind Matt,' said Mum, opening the gate for Ellie. 'You won't come to any harm, I promise you. The surveyor assured us the building's sound where it matters. Just needs a few coats of paint. Matt hasn't learnt to appreciate this place yet.'

Turning to me, she added, 'Talking of safety, I hope you realise there's a lot more of it here than there was among all that city crime and pollution. When did you last breathe real fresh air, or feel you could leave the door unlocked, or see the stars, or hear the silence?'

'Oh, there's plenty of silence in a Ghost Village, believe me,' contributed Ellie as she struggled through the undergrowth on our so-called lawn.

'So?' retorted Mum. 'Then maybe it's time the pair of you livened things up.'

2

Sunday, 15th July

That pest Ellie was on the scene as soon as we'd finished breakfast, tingling her bicycle bell annoyingly in the lane outside. This time she was wearing beige jeans, blue top and a bright red cotton jacket that clashed with her tangled, fiery hair. She hadn't much style, this girl, but then, what could you expect at the back of beyond?

Mum had started painting the kitchen walls and I'd been recruited to do the ceiling. In fact, at that very moment I was crouched on the floor in the open doorway, stirring a tin of 'serene green' emulsion.

'Tell her we're busy!' I growled. I'd had another largely sleepless night and felt anything but sociable. In fact, I'd spent a couple of hours ghost-hunting in the attic but had encountered nothing more sinister than a hole in the roof and an eerie, unseasonable chill.

'Oh, don't be so grumpy, go and see what she wants.' Mum pushed aside a stray lock of 'serene green' hair. 'She's making friendly overtures and it's important for us to get on with our neighbours. I don't want to be cold-shouldered everywhere I go.'

'There's too much to do,' I complained. 'You know you hate ladders and won't tackle the ceiling yourself.'

Mum gazed upwards. 'Actually, I've decided the ceiling's not too bad. It can wait a while. What's more important, we're running out of groceries. Go and ask Ellie if the village shop's open on a Sunday.'

'You ask her.'

'Oh, Matt, for goodness' sake ... '

Sighing, I wiped my hands on a turpentine-soaked rag. There was no arguing with Mum once she'd made up her mind.

To my disgust, it turned out the shop was

indeed open until noon and sold everything from cornflakes to corn plasters.

'Come on, I'll show you where it is,' Ellie offered.

'I'm sure it doesn't need a search party,' I sneered, wheeling out my bike.

'You don't like me, do you?'

'Whatever gave you that idea?' I shovelled on the sarcasm but it still didn't put her off. I guessed she must have a skin like an elephant.

She cycled alongside me, pointing out thrilling sights I would have paid to miss, such as the Golden Feather pub with its washed-out sign and sagging porch, the church and vicarage, well mottled with green mould; the ancient, pocket-sized primary school with a cracked concrete yard, the graffiti-plastered redundant bus shelter; and last of all the post office-cum-general store with its window covered in curling postcard ads.

This, plus a few rows of unprepossessing cottages, was it, the sum total of my new world. I felt trapped, stir-crazy. Mum had had to sell her car to help pay for the move, so escape from this ghostly nightmare would be limited to my pedal-power.

The one decent place I'd spotted was as far out of the village as our place was, though in the other direction: a large, detached villa set well back beyond the church, sensibly trying to pretend it had nothing to do with this riff-raff. It was much bigger than any of the other houses, including ours, and boasted an immaculate garden behind metal gates painted gold. The name on the gates read 'The White House'. Pretentious, or what?

From hints Ellie had dropped I gathered that she lived there but I found it hard to believe. Wishful thinking, I guessed.

'Well, here's the post office, our only shop. Our everything shop, the centre of our universe. Make the most of it, as it's about to close, and when it does this village will really be in a mess. No food, no stamps, no pensions, no bank, no gossip, no nothing.'

Ellie showed me where to prop my bike.

'For anyone with a car, of course, it won't be a problem; just a case of zooming over to Brisco's supermarket in Bansfield. But how many cars have you seen around in this poverty-stricken place?'

When I got back home with the groceries, having managed at last to shake Ellie off, Mum was just finishing a telephone conversation. It was a call she had received, not made, for she hadn't taken time to wipe her hands and the receiver was now serene green. I guessed it must have been Dad, making sure we were settling in okay; nobody else knew our number yet. But I was wrong. Mum welcomed me with that big, false smile of hers, the one she'd worn to tell me about the break-up, and I knew I wouldn't like what she was going to say.

'Guess what – I think I've fixed us up with a lodger,' she blurted out.

'You've *what*?'

'Now, don't go off the deep end, Matt. I know I've sprung this on you, but I didn't expect to manage it so quickly, if at all. I put an advert in a couple of local papers here before we moved, half thinking it would all come to nothing. But there you go – it worked! She's coming tomorrow to look the place over.'

13

'She! Well, once she sees it she'll turn round and run if she has any sense,' I said hopefully.

'I don't think so. She sounded pretty desperate to find somewhere in this area.'

'Well, if she's desperate she's probably in trouble.'

'Rubbish! She's bringing references, and to tell you the truth she's a godsend. We need the money.' After a slight hesitation she added with less confidence, 'But Matt I have to warn you – if she does accept, I'm afraid it means you'll have to move out of the big bedroom and into that spare room above the back porch.'

I was furious.

'Oh Mum! You can't do that! I've just got settled, found places for all my stuff.'

I know I'd complained that my present bedroom was full of draughts and cracked plaster, but it was also huge with two big windows and a whole wall of shelving. I'd never had so much space to myself before, whereas this back room was poky, dark and shelfless.

'What a rotten trick! If you were thinking of doing this you shouldn't have given me the big room in the first place.'

'I told you, I never expected things to move so fast.'

'Much too fast if you ask me; a lodger's the last thing we need.'

'No, Matt, lodgers pay rent. This place may be a bargain, but I've still taken on quite a hefty mortgage. What's more, I've had to buy a new computer, and I'll have to kit you out for this Bansfield Comprehensive next term. So I don't want any more arguments. I'm sorry, but this is the way it has to be, either with this woman or with somebody else.'

I was hopping mad; not least because Mum hadn't consulted me, hadn't thought my opinion worth having. This was my mucked-up life as well as hers.

'Well, if you want stuff reorganised you'll jolly well have to wait,' I sulked childishly. Kicking the spare paint roller into touch I strode off, slammed the kitchen door, grabbed my bike and rode off again. I didn't know where I was heading and I certainly didn't care, provided I didn't bump into that pest Ellie again.

As I passed through the village I did spot her in the distance, cycling in through the White House's golden gates, exchanging chummy waves with a man near the house. So she did live there after all, and for some reason that made me feel even madder.

3

Monday, 16th July

The would-be lodger announced herself as Brenda Voysey. She arrived first thing before we'd even cleared breakfast, and I took an instant dislike to her. For a start, she looked completely out of place here, in a shapeless dark, un-summery top and a calf-length black skirt quite unsuitable for these muddy lanes. In fact, with her matching miserable face she looked as though she'd just come from a funeral. She was thick-set and ungainly, with a sallow complexion, a sharp nose and scraped-back, greying hair. Middle-aged and ugly, was my first reaction.

She had arrived by taxi from Bansfield, asking the driver to collect her again in an hour. At once she directed a keen, searching look at everything with no hint of a smile, although Mum made a great fuss of her, offering refreshments on our best china before giving her the grand tour and outlining the merits of the place.

'We've got breathtaking views, as you can see; one hundred per cent pure air, no light pollution and perfect peace and quiet, all resulting in a gentle yet invigorating pace of life.'

I couldn't help cringing at this fulsome sales pitch; it could have come straight from one of Mum's potboilers.

'Hm! I'd forgotten how isolated the English countryside could make one feel,' Brenda remarked, 'but I need to be in this area for a while. I have some private business to sort out.'

She began asking questions about the village and the neighbours, but Mum explained that we couldn't enlighten her much since Ellie was almost our sole source of information.

'Still, you must have formed an overall

impression of the place,' she insisted. 'Would you say it was a dying community?'

Already dead, I'd have said, but decided I'd better keep quiet. Mum plumped for stimulating and inspiring, which made me cringe some more.

'Yet short of facilities, no doubt?'

Mum turned on one of her smarmy smiles.

'Oh, I think that's a small price to pay, don't you?'

'And what about the house itself? I believe it's been empty for a long time. Have you noticed anything strange about it? Sometimes empty houses develop an atmosphere...'

'Oh, you've been hearing the local gossip,' Mum butted in. 'Nothing to it, I assure you. Just a lot of silly rumours. Don't give them another thought.'

They finally went out to inspect the garden. Brenda pronounced it 'something of a challenge' but said she didn't mind gardening, it was a favourite hobby of hers, and provided we had the proper tools she would be willing to take it on in return for a suitable adjustment to the rent.

That gave Mum something to think about. She steered the woman back into the house for a discussion and my hopes began to rise. After what had been said about our financial straits, Mum would never be persuaded to reduce the rent. Yet when they reappeared I was dismayed to hear Mum saying how well they were going to get on together.

It was a done deal!

Once the odious Brenda had departed, with handshakes but still no smile, I couldn't hide my disgust.

'Oh, come on, Matt! She may not have pop star looks but she's a very nice woman, intelligent, sensible, accommodating, and a gardener to boot. What more could we ask? I can't see you tackling that wilderness out there, and I certainly won't have time.'

'Cold as raw cod, though,' I said with a shiver. 'And what about references?'

'She has three glowing references as a matter of fact. And I wish you'd give her a chance. I suspect there's some great sadness in her life, plus weighty business problems, so you can't expect her to be gushing. I don't see how we could have done any better. A pity it's only a short-term arrangement.'

That last bit was put in to console me, but she needn't have bothered. I was totally inconsolable at the thought of a complete stranger crashing into an already awful situation. I wanted Dad here, not her. Too much was happening too fast. Besides, what business problems could there be to sort out in a place like this?

'She'll ruin your concentration,' I pointed out. 'You know how you hate interruptions when you're writing. Anyway, folks give the most glowing references when they want to get rid of somebody.'

'Those are my problems, not yours. And for goodness' sake cheer up; we're going to be solvent now, with maybe a bit to spare.'

Just as I thought things couldn't get any worse, Mum dropped the final bombshell. Brenda Voysey was actually moving in today, leaving us no time to get used to the idea.

'She's gone to fetch her belongings from Bansfield – apparently she stayed in some hotel there overnight – but she should be back some time this afternoon so we'd better get organised. Perhaps you could make sure you've moved ALL your stuff to the back room before she gets here?'

This was much too much. I began to think seriously of permanent escape. I must have words with Dad, get him on my side. He didn't like us ringing him at his office, but I could catch him tonight as soon as he got home from work. Meantime, I'd make myself scarce. If Mum wanted to annex my bedroom she'd get no help from me.

This time I cycled all the way over a bleak stretch of moorland into this famous Bansfield. Since it called itself a town, maybe it would be civilised enough to run to a snack bar. It was; but the wretched thing was closed. Closed! On a Monday! What a dump!

By the time I reached home again a glazier was busy replacing the cracked windowpane. I hung around watching him for a while, loth to go in and face the music. I'd already passed the departing empty taxi on my way back through the village, so I knew our lodger had arrived.

When I did go in, Mum pounced on me right away.

'Where have you been?' she hissed. 'I thought I asked you to change bedrooms? You really left me in the lurch, Matthew.' (She only called me Matthew when she was really cross.) 'I've had a right old scramble trying to get everything ready. I've had to abandon the painting, and I'm desperate to get the kitchen finished.'

'Why don't you get three-glowing-references Brenda to help you?' I suggested nastily, rushing off upstairs before she could respond.

The draughty, cracked front bedroom, now infinitely desirable, was mine no longer. I peeped through the doorway and saw open suitcases on the floor and clothes strewn across what should have been my bed. Brenda Voysey was already in there, crashing hangers along the wardrobe rail. She didn't acknowledge my presence, though she must have known I was there.

I crossed over to the poky back bedroom, and there was all my gear, thrown higgledy-piggledy everywhere, and the bed not made up. Consumed with fury, I shut myself in there, took out my mobile and rang Dad, working hours or not. There was no reply from his office number, so he must have left early. I tried his new flat but he wasn't there either. I then dialled his mobile number, and this time he answered, but when I said I needed to see him urgently he explained that he was at the airport.

'I'm off to Paris on business. I'll be away for a week or two, possibly more. But don't worry, if we miss our get-together at the end of the month we'll make up for it next time. Didn't Mum tell you about my trip?'

'No, she didn't. Nobody tells me anything,' I growled, switching off in a temper. I felt totally betrayed.

Dad rang me back immediately but I wouldn't answer. Then I heard Mum's phone, so I guessed he'd be quizzing her about the state I was in, hopefully telling her off. I opened the door a crack and tried to listen, but I could only make out a general drone, not what was actually being said. Mum's voice had gone up a few decibels though, so I guessed they were arguing, as usual.

Suddenly it dawned on me how I could escape. If Dad was away, I could stay in his flat by myself. He'd already given me a key to make me feel cool about the arrangement. All I had to do was get there. It was much too far to cycle all the way to Manchester, but I had enough money for train fare. Maybe there was a station in Bansfield. I could cycle over there and hope to work out a route, even if it meant several connections. No time like the present; I'd try tonight, and failing that, I'd try again tomorrow. I knew this was impulsive, but felt that if I didn't make a move now I never would. I'd be trapped forever in this deadly backwater.

I threw some things into a rucksack and slipped out by the front door while Mum was busy preparing supper. I'd ring her when I got to Dad's.

I'd left my bike near the gate, so I was away in seconds, pedalling furiously into the village. The sooner I got to Bansfield, the sooner I could sort out a train.

Unfortunately, Ellie was still around, leaning on her bike on the dried-up patch of grass that calls itself the village green. She was chatting to a desultory-looking gang of teenage lads, but spotted me, called my name, jumped on her bike and caught me up.

'Hi, Matt, where are you off to?'

'You can't come with me.'

That sounded really rude, but I hardened my heart.

'Who says I want to? The gang asked me to introduce you, that's all.'

'Sorry, no time.'

'It won't take a minute, and it's time you met us all. It can't be much fun, stuck out there with just two women in the house.'

So she knew about our visitor!

'Don't miss much, do you?' I sneered.

'Well, it's not hard to keep up to date in a place like this. I couldn't help seeing the taxi when it drove through. We don't get that many taxis, and when it came back the second time I guessed the woman was here to stay. History repeats itself, eh?'

'Well, like I said, I can't hang about here gossiping.'

As I cycled off I could see the gang closing in on her. No doubt they were already tearing me to shreds, but right then I had more urgent problems of my own.

Bansfield had a railway station all right, but clearly it had been closed for years. The decrepit remains of the booking hall were boarded up and covered in graffiti and pigeon droppings. A torn, scribbled-over and almost illegible timetable on the wall dated back to the middle ages. Totally frustrated, I rode into the town centre, hoping there might be a bus instead. I couldn't find a bus station, or even a single stop sign, but at least the snack bar had decided to open by this time. Over refreshments I quizzed the waitress about transport possibilities.

'That your bike outside?' she asked in reply. 'Well, there's your transport possibilities, then. Nothing else but taxis round here.'

Bitterly disappointed, I realised I'd have to go back home. I sat on for a while, gathering strength for the return journey and mourning all this wasted time and effort. Even on a good day, Spelswick to Bansfield was a thirty-minute bike-ride. But then I remembered Ellie's remark about history repeating itself and visions of the sinister Brenda rose before my eyes.

Maybe this effort needn't be wasted after all. I could use it to check up on our lodger. So I asked the waitress for names of local hotels or places to stay the night, and was told there were only two, the Black Bull and Hillview Guest House. I took down the addresses and set out to investigate.

The Black Bull was a down-at-heel sort of place with a rowdy bar and I didn't relish going inside. But I screwed up my courage and negotiated a dark, smelly passageway to the reception desk.

A grouchy woman leaned over the desk and frowned, obviously seeing me as under-age and undesirable.

'What d'you want?'

I explained that I was looking for a Mrs Brenda Voysey.

'She's supposed to be staying here, but she may be checking out soon. I want to catch her before she leaves.'

'Voysey? Nobody of that name here.'

'Has she already left?'

'Never been here.'

'Maybe I didn't pronounce it right.' I spelt it out, just in case.

'Makes no difference what she's called. We've had only men guests for the last two weeks.'

'But I was told...'

'Look, kid, I don't care what you were told. She isn't here, she's never been here and I've never heard of her. Either you're pulling my leg, or somebody's pulling yours. And you're too young to be hanging about on these premises.'

'But would you mind just checking your records, please?'

Now she was getting really cross and ordered me to clear off, so I did.

I fared no better at Hillview Guest House. It was obvious nobody there had heard of Brenda Voysey either, though the woman I spoke to was friendlier and did her best to help.

'Have you tried the Black Bull?' she suggested. 'That's the only other place that takes visitors.'

Well! The Voysey woman had said she didn't know anyone in Bansfield, so she hadn't stayed in a private house. Yet she'd collected luggage from somewhere. I concluded that she'd deliberately chosen to be mysterious and less than truthful. Suddenly there were plenty of facts that needed checking but it was too late to start on them tonight. Since I wasn't now going to Manchester I'd better get home.

Yet late as it was by the time I got back to Spelswick, Ellie was still hanging around, alone this time. She was sitting on the garden wall of Green Lane's end cottage.

'Matt! Wait!' she called, jumping down and running alongside my bike.

I pulled up and got my bit in first.

'What did you mean about history repeating itself?'

'You know what I meant. I told you the

rumours about your house. Don't look so serious; I was only joking. But listen, I drew the short straw to wait for you, and I've wasted enough time sitting here, my bum's gone numb. The message is, we're having a meeting tomorrow morning, nine o'clock on the green, and we want you to be there.'

'Who's "we"?'

'The gang, who else? The ones I wanted to introduce you to. All of us who get bussed into Bansfield Comp., which I suppose is where you'll be going, too?'

'Maybe, if I'm still around next term,' I said, though by then I knew I might well be. For how could I leave Mum on her own with a woman who lied and was not to be trusted? With Dad gone, it was up to me to look out for her, whether I liked it or not, at least until we could sort things out.

'What does your gang want me for, then?'

Ellie grabbed her bike and turned away. 'Oh, they'll explain. Just you be there tomorrow, it's really important.'

As I rode off home I turned for one last glance at Ellie and saw her wheeling her bike in through the gate of the end cottage. Maybe that was where one of the gang lived and she was on her way to report success.

I'd no sooner turned in to our jungle of a garden than the front door flew open and Mum appeared in glorious rage.

'What's the matter with you, storming out without a word? You could at least have warned me you meant to miss supper. Apart from anything else, it was downright rude when you knew Brenda would be eating with us. And what's in the rucksack? Thinking of leaving home, were you, until you got hungry?'

I could have explained that I'd been doing important detective work, discovering that our visitor might not be all she pretended to be. But I wasn't in the mood. I wanted to think about it all carefully before I said anything.

'I've had a long ride and I'm tired. Mind if we save it to the morning?' I pleaded wearily.

4

Tuesday, 17th July

I really had felt weary and fell asleep at once. But I woke at 2 a.m., hearing the moans again. They seemed louder this time, more chilling. I was convinced that somebody or something was on the move. I crept out of bed and mooched around for a while, but there was nothing to see except a line of light under Brenda's bedroom door. So she was awake as well, and muttering to herself – unless she was sobbing or talking in her sleep. She had put an empty suitcase outside her room, probably meaning to move it to the attic later. I shone my torch over it and saw that the initials on the lid were not B.V. but P.W.

Feeling that eerie chill again, I finally went

back to bed and pulled the duvet over my ears, but couldn't get to sleep again. I spent the rest of the night mulling over the events of the last few days and realising that my attitude would have to change.

I obviously couldn't leave Mum now, until I found out what this so-called Brenda was up to, and I might need help, in which case Ellie and her gang might well come in useful. Therefore I'd better make a big effort, go and meet them as requested and try to be sociable after all. I could recruit them to join me in more detective work. Between us we could check out Brenda's background, track down that taxi driver and find out where he'd picked her up, for a start, since it wasn't the Black Bull or Hillview Guest House. Also, as Voysey looked like being a false name we could investigate those initials P.W. If we kept a close eye on the woman, followed her around, chatted her up, listened in on any phone calls, checked the postmarks on her incoming mail . . . I could think of a hundred great ideas in the middle of the night, though they didn't seem so feasible in the morning.

After an uncomfortable breakfast with Mum, I arrived at the green in good time and Ellie introduced me to Ben, Haz, Vern and Katy. I'd caught a glimpse of all four yesterday, of course, but hadn't realised that one of them was a girl. Katy had cropped hair, no curves to speak of and was kitted out like the boys.

At first glance they seemed a miserable lot, not lively enough to be hostile, but slyly cautious all the same. Summing me up, wondering if I was worth the trouble. Especially Vern, the wariest and most miserable of the lot, who had stepped defensively in front of a bagful of beer cans, though he must have known I'd seen them.

The one called Ben – the best-looking and probably the oldest – seemed to be the ringleader and fired off some pretty personal questions, such as why had we moved here, had we bought or rented, and how long were we intending to stay. I kept trying to butt in with a well-prepared request for their help, but before I could manage it I found they were asking for mine.

'Well, look – Ellie had a bright idea. She thought your turning up might come in useful to help with something we're planning,' Ben explained at last. 'But you'd need to keep it a secret.'

'I think I might just manage that.'

'Well, what it is – we're fixing a bit of a surprise inside the church, so we need to get rid of the vicar for a while. It's going to take time to set it all up and it wouldn't do for Rev. Watts to come barging in at the wrong moment.'

'Yeah, ruin everything, that would,' said Haz, winking at Ellie.

'So we want you to persuade your mum to invite the Rev. for a meal tomorrow night. Get him right out of the way.'

'No five-minute chats over a cup of tea,' insisted Katy, who had a permanent scowl, especially for Haz, and a massive chip on her shoulder about something. 'It has to be a proper meal that takes up a couple of hours at least. He mustn't come back before dark.'

'You WHAT?'

This was the last thing I'd expected and I

must have looked pretty astonished as one by one they suddenly loosened up and bombarded me with details.

'No last minute hitches. Make sure the Rev. turns up on time.'

'Say, seven-thirty till ten.'

'Ask him loads of questions. That'll fill the time in, keep him hanging on.'

'Yeah, tell him you're keen to get to know all about the village, who's who and what's what. Lay it on thick.'

'Steady on!' I managed to butt in at last. 'You must be joking. We've only just finished unpacking. The paint's still wet in the kitchen and my mum's the worst cook in Britain. She won't be wanting guests in a hurry.'

'I heard she'd just got one,' mumbled Vern.

'That's different; she's the lodger. Anyway, my mother wouldn't invite a vicar, of all people. She may know her way around the Bible,' I said with a meaningful stare at Ellie, 'but I promise you she's an out-and-out heathen.'

'Great! You tell him that. Best way to fetch him at the double,' grinned Haz. 'He'll be raring to convert her.'

'You don't know my mother. She'd be more likely to convert him.'

'Well, we need to get on,' snapped Katy. 'Look at it as a social thing – nothing to do with religion. What time do you usually eat?'

'You can't be serious!' I cried.

'Deadly serious,' Ben confirmed, and he looked it.

'Not to worry,' Ellie beamed brightly. 'I bet I can persuade your mum. I get on fine with her. I'll come home with you, turn on my charm.'

'Oh, no you won't! My mother stays out of this – unless you fill me in with every last detail of what you're planning. For all I know it could be something illegal, like burning down the church or desecrating the altar. Or are you just planning a booze-up and private orgy in the vestry?'

There was a pregnant silence while they gave one another significant glances. Then Ben the boss spoke up.

'All right, I suppose it's only fair to let you in on it properly. Follow me.'

He led me behind the church to where a decrepit wooden hut sagged crazily towards complete collapse. Ben gave it a kick on its way and the door, already hanging loose, fell to the ground and split into several pieces.

'See that? That was our club, our meeting place, our hideout. The sole spot where we could get together in private. There's nowhere else. So you see what we're up against? If we don't do something drastic our lives won't be worth living. The only answer is a campaign to save this rapidly vanishing village. You haven't been here long enough to realise what a total mess we're in, but if you're intending to stay you'll soon be in the thick of it as well. The whole place is falling apart, just like this.'

He gave another kick and this time the hut collapsed entirely, bits flying off in all directions under a rising cloud of dust.

The others had followed us and now looked more fed up than ever.

'We're marooned,' moaned Vern. 'No trains, no buses except for our special school bus, and even that's so clapped out it's always breaking down.'

'And you'll have noticed the post office is closing next week,' added Haz. 'Talk about dire! That shop's our lifeline.'

'Don't forget the primary school,' mourned Katy. 'My kid sister Fran goes there – WENT there, pardon me! Only fifteen pupils now, so they reckon it's not economic to keep it open any more. It closed this summer, which means from September all the kids will have to go to Bansfield Primary and share our clapped-out bus. Ever been on a travelling zoo? And I'll be expected to mother our Fran, the little demon, as if babysitting through the holidays wasn't bad enough.'

Charming, I thought, talking about your little sister like that!

By this time we were ambling back to the green and they were each adding more and more misery to the tally.

'But this is the worst, having no leisure facilities, nowhere to meet in bad weather. Our folks aren't keen on having us all in the house at once.'

'I wonder why?' grinned Katy, prodding the beer cans with her foot.

'It's a miracle we haven't forgotten how to read. We used to have a mobile library once a fortnight but now that's stopped coming as well.'

'It's not a life here, it's an existence,' Vern added bitterly. 'And when you finally leave school the only jobs round here are in near-bankrupt farming.'

'Nowhere to live when you want to set up house for yourself.'

'In fact, a big, fat nothing.'

'Sounds pretty grim,' I agreed, 'but short of moving away there's not much you can do about it.'

'Well, that's enough moaning for now,' Ben cut in. 'In case you lot have lost sight of the goalpost, there IS something we can do. Plenty of publicity, that's what we're after, remember?'

Turning to me, he added, 'So this is where you come in, helping our church surprise. We've been waiting ages for a plausible way to get rid of the vicar for an evening, and you

41

and your mum can do that for us. We're going to chain ourselves to the pews. So now you know – and you're sworn to secrecy.'

I couldn't help grinning. What sort of kids' stuff was that?

'What else can we do? We've no choice!' Katy snapped, noting my amusement. 'We have to make it something outrageous, it's our only chance of real publicity. We'll ring the Bansfield rag on a mobile when we're ready. Once their editor catches on we're hoping the news will spread like fireweed.'

For the first time she showed a spark of life.

'Who knows? Before you can say God we'll have reporters descending on us from every-where, maybe even a telly crew.'

'We just need to be listened to,' added Ben more soberly. 'Raise a massive cry for help. And if that doesn't make a difference I don't know what will.'

'Television crews? Don't you think that's a bit ambitious?' I mocked, but I could see they weren't pleased.

'What's wrong with ambitious?'

'Ambitious starts with proper planning.

Chaining yourselves to church pews can't be easy. Have you tried it out?' I asked. 'Besides, even if you managed it, the police would simply come along, cut through the chains, read you the riot act and that would be that. At the worst you might get done for trespass, but even that's dubious in a church. They're supposed to be open for everyone, places of sanctuary even. You might end up with a stint of community service for damaging the pews, which would be boring for you, but not exactly mind-blowing headlines. It would all be forgotten in a couple of days.'

'Oh, isn't he the clever one?' sneered Vern, while Katy muttered viciously that it was none of my business what they did.

'Really? I thought you were relying on my mum to decoy the vicar.'

'I told you we shouldn't have involved him,' grumbled Vern. 'He's a townie. What does he know?'

'I know a better way to get maximum publicity,' I insisted. 'What you need is mystery. Build up the suspense. Start a scare that leads to a major panic. Get everybody wondering what's going on. Keep 'em on tenterhooks for days.'

'What sort of scare?'

'Vanish! All of you leave the village together. Disappear.'

That had been my planned solution; why not theirs?

'You know – a modern Pied Piper kind of story,' I went on. 'Strip the village of its youth. Get everybody making wild guesses as to where and why you've gone. And think of the search they'd organise! Great pics and headlines! Long lines of police searching over the moors! With a bit of luck you might even get a question asked in Parliament.'

'Oh, yeah!' Ben retorted bitterly. 'Disappear? Where to?'

'To my dad's flat in Manchester. He's away for a few weeks and I've got the key. All you'd have to find would be travel costs – communal taxi to the nearest train, wherever that might be – and a few sleeping bags.'

And if they messed the place up it would serve Dad right for not being there when I needed him.

'He's nuts!' snarled Vern, spitting viciously into the duck-pond.

'Fifty miles to the nearest station! Does he think taxi fares grow on trees?'

Haz and Katy added more disgusted remarks, though I noticed Ellie kept quiet.

Then Ben said, 'Look, we don't want criticism or harebrained, useless ideas; we just want some practical help with the plan we've already made. We've put a lot of thought into it. You let us worry about the end result, which might be more spectacular than you think. Just decide whether you're with us or not.'

'Sure I'm with you,' I shrugged. 'I'm just as fed up with this place as you are. But the offer of the flat still stands. You'd be mad not to accept. Think it over.'

I felt disappointed, frustrated, jealous. What gave this Ben the idea that he was the only one with brains? And why were the others too thick to recognise my superior plan? Still, I wanted to keep in with them for my own benefit. Maybe if I left them to discuss it they'd change their minds. So I cycled off.

Ellie soon caught up with me.

'Hey, wait! We need to tackle your mum right away.'

'Waste of time,' I warned. But I was wrong.

It took Ellie less than twenty minutes to twist my mum round her little finger. She told her the vicar was dying to meet us, that he expected incomers to invite him round as soon as possible so that he could make them feel at home. It was tradition, and he would be hurt if we broke the pattern. Anyway, he could fill us in about the history of the house.

I suspect it was this last bit which really did the trick. That, and the fact that Mum never guessed we were the only incomers for a couple of decades. I knew she was keen to make connections, though. So she finally did agree to issue a supper invitation, but not until Saturday, as she needed time to smarten the place up a bit more.

'Why don't you come too, Ellie?' she offered. 'You could introduce us all, break the ice. And you'd be company for Matt.'

'Thanks, I'd love to, but unfortunately I

have another appointment on Saturday,' said Ellie, smirking at me behind Mum's back.

As soon as Mum went off to fetch refreshments Ellie gave a little whoop of triumph.

'I told you she'd do it! Saturday's better than nothing. After all, we've got five weeks' holiday left so there's no great rush. It's just the boys who get so impatient.'

My disappointment trebled and turned into childish resentment. Now I'd never persuade them to go to Manchester. Why hadn't they leapt at the sheer brilliance of my generous idea?

'Well, I hope you aren't expecting me to chain myself up with the rest of you,' I muttered sulkily.

'No way! Your job is to help entertain Rev. Watts and make sure he doesn't leave too early. Good thing you turned up. He's hard to tempt out in an evening.'

We had just finished our snack and were preparing to leave when our lodger walked into the room, submitting Ellie at once to her usual peering scrutiny. Maybe she'd guessed why Ellie was here, and was about to throw a spanner in the works. So I scooped Ellie out through the door as fast as I could.

'What's the hurry? Not going to introduce me to your spooky lodger, then?' grinned Ellie. 'She's pretty weird, I must say. That icy stare gave me the creeps. A ghostly presence – what did I tell you?'

'Oh, come on! You're not still chewing that old cud?'

Ellie grinned wickedly. 'Think she's pregnant under that shapeless black skirt?'

'Don't be ridiculous, she's a bit old for that.'

'Good at guessing ages, are you? Anyway, I don't take to her, and neither did the folks who saw her hanging around the village yesterday. Katy's gran said she thought she recognised her from somewhere long ago but couldn't think where. Everybody said she was asking too many questions. So don't you tell her what we're up to.'

'She won't hear anything from me. I promised secrecy, didn't I?'

Ellie sighed. 'Secrets aren't always easy to keep. Some folks can winkle them out of you. Still, if she eats with you on Saturday, you can keep an eye on her. Better than having her nosy-parkering round the village.'

'Oh, take care you don't show any gratitude for all our trouble,' I warned that exasperating girl.

The minute I went back into the house I heard my matchmaking mother explaining to Brenda with a saucy grin that Eloise was my 'special' friend and that we'd be in the same year group at school next term.

(Special friend? Special bugbear, more like.)

'She lives at the White House, didn't you say, Matt?'

'Really? Well, that IS a surprise!' exclaimed Brenda. She was obviously thinking what I'd thought myself, that Ellie didn't seem to belong to a posh place like that. But funnily enough, I found I resented this woman making snap judgments about Ellie, bugbear or not. She hardly knew the girl. I might well have said something rude, but by then Mum was starting to panic about Saturday.

'Better make a start on the garden, I suppose,' she hinted, before dragging me off into the kitchen to plan a menu and write out shopping lists.

'You know what – I'm quite looking forward to sparring with a vicar. And the meal needn't cost much; they're usually vegetarians, aren't they?'

By the time we'd talked that through, Brenda was actually oiling the lawn mower.

5

Wednesday, 18th July

Again I awoke in the middle of the night. Twenty past two, the alarm clock said. This time the noises sounded more substantial, and I knew for certain that our lodger was on the move. I heard her room door creak open, then her footsteps padding along the landing. Mum always insisted on leaving the stairs' light on during the night, so I could see Brenda quite clearly. She could have been heading for the bathroom, but in fact she was starting downstairs.

I crept carefully after her. She went into the kitchen, turned on the light, opened the fridge, poured herself a glass of milk and sat at the table with a book and some papers. It was pretty chilly hanging about, peering through a crack in the partly-open kitchen door. I had just decided to sneak back into my nice warm bed when she stood up, collected her things and started towards me. There was a larder to the left of the kitchen door, so I slipped into there to let her go past me up the stairs. When I was sure she was back in her room I made a move. But as I passed the kitchen I saw that a white envelope had fallen to the floor. I picked it up – to return it, of course, but not before I'd studied it in my room.

In the envelope I found a carefully-drawn and detailed plan headed 'The White House' and at the bottom was scribbled the one word 'Ellie?' There was also a photograph of a woman resembling Brenda and holding a child. On the back of that was scribbled the name 'Perdita'.

I sat for a while, staring thoughtfully at these papers. Had Brenda been casing the joint, ready to burgle the White House? Or maybe to kidnap Ellie? Or both? And who was Perdita?

All this was odd by any standards, but added to my other discoveries it seemed positively disturbing. For now not only my mother, but Ellie too, might be under threat.

As soon as I could after breakfast I cycled into the village, hoping to pass on a warning. The gang had already congregated at their usual spot on the green, and I wasted no time in telling them that I thought Ellie was being spied on.

'Our lodger's pretty interested in Ellie's house,' I said. 'She's drawn a plan of it, with Ellie's name at the bottom.'

'So what?' said Ben. 'She can draw what she likes. It's a free country.'

'But don't you think it's a bit odd?'

'Not specially.'

'Well, there's more.'

Yesterday they had all been so taken up with their own problems that I hadn't had a chance to mention mine, but now I let them in on my detective work as well.

'So you see, that woman's been lying about all sorts of things. She's up to something, and I reckon she might be dangerous. She's come here for a special reason. Could it be something to do with your family, Ellie?'

Ellie laughed. ''Course not! Why me?' All the same, I thought she looked uneasy.

'Does anybody in the village know anything about her?' I persisted.

Ellie shrugged. 'They're all making wild guesses. She doesn't give much away. My gran said she looked vaguely familiar but she couldn't really place her.'

'Mum overheard something in the post office,' admitted Ben. 'She reckons Brenda's come into a load of dosh recently; won the lottery or something.'

'Robbed a bank, more like.'

'Oh, I can just picture that!' I sneered.

'Conned some unsuspecting pensioners out of their life savings, then?'

'Not round here, she hasn't, they've got none. Anyway, Matt, if she's so flush you should get your mum to put the rent up.'

'We saw her coming out of the estate agent's in Bansfield, didn't we, Haz?'

'Could be planning to buy you out, then, Matt.'

I shook my head. 'Over my mum's dead body.'

'Hey! Careful what you say!' They all seemed to find this funny.

'Well, why don't we do some serious digging?' I said. 'For a start, is there anyone round here with a surname beginning with W?'

'Only Rev. Watts.'

'Well, you just be careful,' I warned Ellie. 'Stick close to the others.'

'No problem there,' said Haz, giving Ellie a protective squeeze.

So then I asked them outright if they'd help me with further checks on Brenda, starting with the taxi driver. But they didn't exactly leap to the rescue. I suppose they were mad at Mum for making them wait until Saturday.

Ellie was the only one to respond.

'Oh, you'll soon track him down. There's just the one taxi firm in Bansfield. It's called Red Line, has an office at the top of the High Street. You can't miss it.'

She didn't volunteer to check it out for

me, though. None of them did. In fact, Ben chipped in to say they were just off to the churchyard to check over their plans.

'Can't leave anything to chance, even though we HAVE got more time than we need.'

That was me snubbed and disposed of! Clearly they weren't going to help me, then. So I set off for Bansfield once more – on my own, and resenting the fact that this business of helping out wasn't mutual.

Still, thanks to Ellie's directions, I soon spotted the taxi office with its huge sign over the waiting room door. A girl sat behind a sliding glass screen monitoring calls, and two women customers were chatting on a bench.

'Take a seat,' the girl told me. 'Ten minutes' wait, okay?'

I would have explained what I wanted, but her phone rang just then and she was immediately caught up in complex arrangements. So I sat.

A few minutes later a car pulled up outside and a taxi driver walked in. I recognised him at once, and although he had come to collect the two women I followed them out and grabbed his attention. Did he remember taking a fare to Spelswick last Monday, I asked him – a female fare who wanted him to collect her again in an hour? He did remember, but when I asked where he picked her up, he said, 'Here at the office, of course.'

He started to walk away but I stopped him again.

'But do you know where she came from before that?'

'What's it to you?'

'She – she's ill,' I improvised. 'We're trying to trace her relatives.'

I was sure he didn't believe me, but he added grudgingly that she'd turned up in another taxi – a Walverton cab.

'She was heading for Spelswick eventually, but had some sort of a call to make in Bansfield first, so she broke her journey here. The Walverton bloke had another booking to collect and couldn't wait, so I offered to take her on. Now clear off, I'm busy.'

After he'd gone I asked the girl in the office to give me names and numbers of taxi firms in Walverton so I could ring them on my mobile.

'No need,' she said. 'I couldn't help overhearing, and I can tell you what you want to know. I remember that woman – funny looker dressed in black. She dropped off here to make a call somewhere and dumped her luggage on me. Then she made a trip to Spelswick, came back for her luggage, then zoomed off to Spelswick again. Quite a carry-on! The Walverton driver who dropped her off is a friend of mine so he stopped to say hello. He warned me to keep an eye on her because he'd picked her up outside Walverton Women's Prison.'

It was a shock, but I was sure she was telling the truth; it all fitted in with my growing suspicions. So I couldn't get home fast enough, being desperate to warn Mum right away. I'd never cycled so fast in my life.

Yet when I finally blurted it all out, my exasperating mother simply smiled and said, 'So what? Even if what you are thinking is true, she must have served her time and now she's entitled to a fresh start.'

'Brenda Voysey's bound to be a false name,' I pointed out, adding the evidence of the suitcase initials and the envelope, but Mum didn't mind that either.

'She might have thought it wiser to change her name. It isn't easy making a fresh start. Some people are very inquisitive, not to mention cruel. We're all entitled to our privacy.'

When I showed her the photograph she agreed that the woman did look like Brenda.

'Perdita's such a sad name,' she sighed. 'It means "lost".'

'We're the ones who've lost. What about those references? They can't be genuine and I bet you didn't check them. Surely you'll have to get rid of her now?'

'I certainly will not,' retorted Mum indignantly. 'She's company for me, she's working wonders in the garden, and I was hoping I'd brought you up to be more compassionate than that, Matthew Padstow. Now, come and give me a hand in the kitchen, and make sure you return those papers.'

6

Thursday, 19th July

Having spent the rest of yesterday on boring domestic chores, I was thankful to escape this morning. Mum had detailed me to deliver a formal invitation to the vicar, tricked out in her best calligraphy.

I cycled over to the green, and there was Ellie sitting on the grass by herself. Today she looked as depressed as I felt, but this wasn't her usual mood, so I wondered if sinister Brenda was the cause.

I felt obliged to emphasise my previous warning, so I settled down beside her and steered the conversation round to our lodger.

'Are you sure you don't know her? What if I told you she might have a prison record?

Or a daughter? Or might be called Perdita Something-beginning-with-W? She's got a weird interest in your house. Aren't you worried?'

'I've got better things to worry about than your lodger.'

'Such as?'

'None of your business.'

'Well look, I'm just off to the vicarage with this invitation Mum's insisted on. She wants him to have the time in writing, so he doesn't turn up too early. Why don't you come with me to cheer yourself up?'

'Can't, I'm meeting Haz in a minute.'

'Suit yourself!'

So I tackled the vicarage alone, feeling annoyed because she hadn't appreciated the thawing animosity I'd worked so hard on – and that she obviously preferred Haz's company. What on earth did she see in him? With his burgeoning acne and permanent slouch he wasn't even blessed with looks, never mind personality.

I already knew that Ben's mother was the vicar's part-time housekeeper, and it was she who opened the door when I rang.

'Vicar's in the church,' she told me, so I went across there and wandered in.

It was pretty gloomy inside, but I could see at once that the gang's famous plan wasn't going to work. There was no way anyone would be able to chain themselves to these pews because they all had solid backs. I'd imagined some sort of regular carved gaps in the woodwork, so that chains could be slotted through. I was amazed that nobody had thought of this snag already.

As soon as I'd issued the eagerly-accepted invitation I hurried back to the green. Ellie was still there – ha! So spotty Haz had stood her up! – and I blurted out my opinion of the pews, dying to say 'I told you so!'

Whatever reaction I'd expected it wasn't the one I got. Ellie simply sighed and said, 'Okay, so you've found us out.'

'What do you mean?'

'We never intended to chain ourselves to the pews. We knew it wouldn't work, and we've got no chains anyway. We just told you that to put you off the scent.'

I was furious. 'Well, of all the blasted cheek! You mean to say you're letting my mother lay on this rotten meal and go to all sorts of trouble, worry and EXPENSE SHE CAN ILL AFFORD – for nothing?'

'Oh, keep your hair on! It isn't for nothing. We still need to get rid of the vicar. Only the surprise we're planning isn't quite what you thought it was.'

'I knew it!' I yelled. 'You're going to do something really daft, land yourselves in serious trouble, and I'll be up to my neck in it as well for helping you.'

Ellie grabbed my arm and swung me round to face her.

'All right, look! You're a bad-tempered so-and-so, but I suppose you've a right to go off the deep end; we've treated you pretty badly. But if you'll calm down I'll put you in the picture. I wanted to tell you a proper tale in the first place but the others wouldn't let me, which was mean after all you've done. So here goes – but for goodness' sake don't let on that I've spilled the beans.'

She paused and took a deep breath before

adding, 'On Saturday night, when the vicar's at your's, we're going to break into the church tower. Ben can pinch the keys from his mum who works for the vicar. We're going to climb to the top and stand on the edge of the parapet in a line, holding lanterns, and Ben's going to shout our demands through a megaphone. Maybe we'll let off a few fireworks as well. Then when we've raised a crowd and got everyone's attention we'll threaten to throw ourselves off the edge, one by one, unless some definite promises of village improvements are forthcoming. And if you breathe a word of this your life won't be worth living, believe me.'

I was thunderstruck; couldn't come up with anything less moronic than 'Hell's bells!'

Haz turned up before I'd recovered my wits, or I might have heard the worst bit of the story there and then. But he made it obvious that I was in the way, so I left them to it – with my brain turning somersaults.

Almost immediately I ran into Vern. Maybe, with a bit of careful questioning, I could squeeze a few more details out of him.

'Fancy showing me around?' I asked.

'What's to show?'

'Places to go; walks and that,' I said lamely.

'Up one lane, down another. Couldn't be simpler.'

'There must be more to it than that. All this countryside...'

'Look, I don't know what you're after, but I'm not the least bit interested. I hate this place. I'd get the hell out of it if I could, but I'm stuck here more than most.'

'Can't be that bad, surely?'

'What do YOU know?'

'I know this: that I'm fed up as well, but it's even worse for me. What you've never had you never miss, but imagine what it's like, swapping city life for this dump; giving up shops, cinemas, theatres, clubs, coffee bars – and that's just for starters. Still, I don't intend to let it grind me down.'

'Then you're a stupid fool!'

'Maybe. But I reckon you can either settle for what you've got or try to do something about it.'

'Well, if you're intending to stop here you'd be better off dead. I really mean that.'

'No, you don't. Nothing's that bad.'

We argued on for quite a while; or at least I argued and Vern just took to grunting a few disparaging retorts. Plainly he was a lot more depressed than I was, and ungracious with it. Besides, he told me nothing I wanted to know. In the end I gave up and went home.

Brenda was working on the garden. She had cleared a huge space near the back wall and actually managed to look pleased with herself.

'What do you think? Is it starting to look more civilised?' she asked.

'Well, you couldn't make it any worse than it was.'

Brenda shrugged. 'That's what happens when Nature takes over. Those brambles I've just cleared away had completely smothered the little cherry tree that used to light up that corner. It's dead now, such a pity.'

I had actually reached my room before I realised what she'd said. How did she know how that cherry tree used to look?

7

Friday, 20th July

This morning, when I managed to get Ellie by herself again, I soon began to realise that I hadn't heard the half of their crackbrained plan.

I began by trying to talk her out of the whole stupid scheme.

'Do you want to give us all heart attacks? That tower looks as though it will soon be a crumbling wreck. However careful you are, one of you might slip and fall, or just the weight of you lot tramping about could fetch the whole thing down. As for letting fireworks off up there...'

'Yeah, yeah, we've thought of all that,' she snapped impatiently. 'And if you must know,

I'm not exactly looking forward to it. I haven't much of a head for heights. But we all promised to stick together, and that's important. Vital, in fact.'

There was a long pause before she added, 'Trouble is, I've found out something much more serious. One of us might just be playing it for real.'

What did she mean? That one of them might actually JUMP?

'Well – go on!'

Ellie, it seemed, had begun to suspect that Vern fancied himself as a martyr.

'He's a brooder, our Vernon. Takes things to heart; thinks too much.'

'Don't we all, in a place like this?'

'Not like him. You know what the news bulletins are like these days, brimful of terrorists, suicide bombers, the lot. Every time you turn the telly on there's a blown-up bus or embassy or whatever, and a screen full of bodies. Vern's obsessed with it all. He collects news cuttings, has an album full. He's even filled a display board on his bedroom wall. Not with pictures of the gruesome carnage – I don't mean that – but with all sorts of articles about what makes these monsters tick. They – and even their families and friends – always seem certain they're right, and Vern laps it up. He sees them as self-sacrificing heroes working for a genuine cause with tempting visions of a wonderful afterlife. I shouldn't be telling you this, and you're dead meat if you breathe a word. But I'm pretty sure Vern's convinced himself that sacrificing a life for a good cause is really worthwhile.'

And he believed ours was a good cause!

I was gobsmacked. Vern hadn't struck me as a religious fanatic. No wonder Ellie was looking so miserable, with a secret like that on her conscience.

'Oh, he can't be serious!' I cried hopefully. 'He's just trying to impress you.'

'That's easy for you to say, but poor old Vern's had a rough time lately. His mum died last year, and he took that really hard, they were very close. Then his dad got made redundant, and as if that wasn't bad enough, he followed it up with a nasty accident, helping out on one of the farms. He actually lost his foot. Been on crutches ever since. There aren't any cushy sit-down office jobs round here, so he's unemployable, which means Vern has to help out with a Saturday job on a farm, and he hates it. What's more, his dad's told him he'll have to leave school the minute he's old enough and work on the farm full time, which is a real shame as he's brighter than any of us. Uni material, the teachers reckon. Farming's the last thing he wants to do, but it's all that's on offer if you've no qualifications. So what with one thing and another, poor old Vern's really gutted.'

'Brighter than any of you? I wouldn't call it bright, committing suicide in front of a crowd of friends and neighbours.'

Ellie looked a bit shamefaced. 'I don't say he will. I just know that's the way his mind's working, and he'll not be shifted with words. He's even into some suicide chat-room on the Internet. I daren't tell Ben and the others or they'll stop Vern coming with us, but if that happens he might just go up the tower by himself another time, or do

70

something just as daft. At least if we're all there together we can keep an eye on him. I'm hoping he'll bottle out anyway when he sees how far down it is.' Ellie shuddered at the thought.

'But you can't risk it!'

'So what do we do? You tell me. You reckon you're the one with all the stunning ideas.'

Strangely enough, I felt I'd have given anything to impress Ellie just then, but this problem needed mature consideration. Whilst I was trying to give it some, Haz and Vern turned up. Haz was looking for Ellie as usual and obviously couldn't wait to start smooching. So I seized my chance and hauled Vern aside. Ellie might not be able to talk him round, but I was pretty sure I could.

Best idea seemed to be to invite him home, get him away from the others. So I asked for some decorating advice, plus a bit of practical help.

'Why pick on me?'

'Well, Ben's up to the ears in plans, Haz and Ellie are all over each other and Katy has to hang around to keep an eye on her kid sister. Which leaves you. Ellie tells me you're good at D.I.Y.'

'Yeah, well I've had to be,' he grunted sulkily.

'Tomorrow morning then, nine o'clock sharp?'

He gave me a look of utter disgust before walking away. Then I remembered that he did farm work on Saturdays.

8

Saturday, 21st July

So of course Vern didn't turn up. I waited a while, just in case, then cycled over to his house. I rang the bell a couple of times and his dad opened the door eventually, struggling with his crutches. He confirmed that Vern was over at Stemson's farm, so I asked for directions, then went back home to put together a packed lunch. Vern would have to break for food at some point, and even if he'd taken some with him we could still picnic together.

On the way home I ran into another problem. I spotted Brenda Voysey walking up the path through the White House garden, bold as a banner headline.

I hung around to see what she was up to this

time. She rang the bell and a man opened the door, inviting her in with a handshake and a friendly smile. Could that be Ellie's dad? I realised I didn't know much about Ellie's family, except that she was an only child. But she'd said she didn't know Brenda, so what could the woman want with Ellie's folks? And why had she made that detailed plan of the house?

Life was rapidly becoming more and more complicated. With two of them to look out for – three, if you counted Mum – I'd have to keep my wits about me. First I needed a good excuse for missing that dinner with the vicar – Mum would hardly get herself murdered in front of him – for now I had no alternative but to climb that tower with the rest of them, if they'd let me.

I rang Ellie's mobile and discovered that she'd gone off to Bansfield for the day with Haz. Well then, at least she and Vern were both out of harm's way for the time being, which gave me some breathing space, plus time for a few chores as a sweetener for Mum in view of tonight's betrayal.

Some sweetener! Mum blew her top when I said I was having an evening out.

'Ellie's lot are throwing a party,' I explained. (Well, it was a party of sorts, a fireworks party.) 'That's why she couldn't come to ours. And you're always nagging me to be nice to her and make new friends, so I thought I'd join them.'

'Oh, very convenient! Look, Matthew, this meal was your idea. You can't just waltz off and leave me to it.'

'Actually it was Ellie's idea,' I pointed out. 'Anyway, you don't need me; you want some proper adult conversation. The vicar might come up with some weird info about this house that he wouldn't tell in front of me. You could well end up with volumes of best-selling ideas that'll make your fortune. And you'll have three-references-Brenda for backup.'

Before she could say any more I slipped neatly away to Stemson's farm with my picnic lunch.

Vern, up to the wellies in muck, didn't seem pleased to see me and said he hadn't time to stop, as in view of the evening's plans he wanted to finish early. I managed to persuade him that he'd work all the faster with some food inside him. So eventually I got him to sit on a wall and share my sandwiches.

'Ellie tells me the teachers have you marked out for uni,' I said chattily.

He gave a disgusted grunt. 'Think my dad could manage that, letting me run up massive debts while he struggled on his own? Anyway, I don't believe in planning for the future. The present is more than enough to cope with.'

'Everybody plans for the future,' I said.

'No, they don't. At least, not in the way you think. Some people know perfectly well that they haven't got a personal future of their own.'

'You mean folk who are terminally ill?'

'Folk who see a need to give up their own future for other people's good.'

'Like what? Caring for sick relatives? Becoming nuns or missionaries? That's still a future.'

I could see he was getting rattled.

'You haven't a clue!' he sneered. 'You're just like the rest of them, self-centred and blinkered and – and – trivial.' He had some trouble finding that last word.

'Hey, steady on!' I protested. 'I can't be that bad. I'm "self-centred" enough to be concerned about you, for a start. And generous; you've just eaten half my lunch.'

'Only to stop you nagging. I need to stay calm today, keep a clear head.'

'Does it need a clear head, then, to chain yourself to a pew?'

Vern gave me a thunderous look. 'You know perfectly well that's not what we're doing. Ellie's told you all about it, hasn't she? Can't keep anything to herself, that girl. I knew I shouldn't have trusted her. She's sent you to pep-talk me, hasn't she? Well, you're wasting your time.'

'And you could be wasting a lot more than that.'

'Uni isn't that marvellous,' he sneered, deliberately misunderstanding me.

'Have you thought about your friends and family? They'd be devastated.'

'Just because I didn't get a stupid degree? You must be joking!'

By then I was losing my rag.

'NO! Because they saw you smashing your-self up among the gravestones,' I yelled recklessly.

Vern was furious. 'Mind your own bloody business!' He leapt up and hurled the rest of his sandwich at me. 'If I wanted to jump I'd jump, and nothing you could say would stop me.'

By half past seven we were straining at the leash. We had gathered round the back of the church with Katy as lookout, waiting for Rev. Watts to leave the vicarage. Despite Mum's carefully-worded invitation, he was late; it was nearly eight o'clock before Katy signalled that he was finally on his way to ours, so we could make a move.

There had been some argument about me joining the expedition, but between us Ellie and I had managed to convince the others that I'd be an asset.

'If a newcomer can see the problems of this village already and show solidarity with us, that'll make even more of an impression,' Ellie had insisted, though she knew perfectly well why I was there.

Ben produced the keys to the tower and we all sneaked in.

'Guess what – I saw Brenda Voysey shake hands with your dad,' I muttered to Ellie as we started our climb. It was the first chance I'd had to pass on my latest fears.

'So? You said she was keen on gardening.'

'What's that got to do with it?'

'My dad's the gardener at the White House. I thought you knew. I'm sure I must have mentioned it.'

'You mean – you don't live there?'

Ellie laughed. 'Live there? Chance'd be a fine thing! I get to snoop round the green-houses now and then when the Colonel's away, but that's about it.'

I felt suddenly confused. 'Where do you live, then?'

'End cottage, Green Lane.'

The one I'd seen her going into when I'd thought she was reporting back to one of the others.

'Then what's our Brenda doing at the White House?'

'How should I know? Maybe she's cadging some plants for your garden. Or maybe she's going to buy the place. It's up for sale; the Colonel's moving to Scotland, and who can blame him?'

'Keep quiet, you two!' Ben hissed from up ahead. So I was left with this unsolved puzzle whizzing round my brain, along with all the other worries.

I couldn't help noticing that Vern had scrubbed up pretty well for the occasion. He was wearing blinding white trainers and T-shirt with well-laundered jeans and had washed his hair. Obviously wanted to look his best on the mortuary slab.

I tried to make eye contact with Vern, but he kept his gaze well down at ground level. Mind you, nobody was very chummy; we were all too uptight with last-minute nerves.

Ben had made us fill backpacks with lanterns, torches, banners and endless other stuff he'd decided we might need. My load was quite heavy and threatened to throw me off balance as we mounted the worn stone spiral stairs. I was relieved when we reached the top. But then, wriggling out through the trap door onto the walkway, I suddenly realised how windy it was up there. The whole tower seemed to be swaying. As I inched my way along the rotting boards I could feel my heart racing. I was suddenly more anxious than I'd ever felt in my whole life. What was I doing up here? I almost wished I'd stayed at home swapping platitudes with the vicar.

By the time we'd arranged a line of lanterns along the parapet we were definitely a sight to be seen. Ellie and Haz had unfurled a long, white banner made from a bedsheet which read: SAVE OUR VANISHING GHOST VILLAGE OR WE'LL HAUNT YOU FOR-EVER! They had quite a struggle to fix it in place and had to be content to leave it flapping wildly in the wind.

Then Ben yelled into the megaphone: 'Attention! Attention! Villagers of Spelswick gather round!' After several repeats of this he began to raise an audience. Doors opened here and there along the lanes. Some people came out, saw what was happening and spread the news to their neighbours. Soon there was a growing group of adults and children converging on the churchyard, shouting and gesturing. Their noise even drew spectators from the mouldy old Golden Feather.

'Great! We're doing great!' Ben encouraged us. 'Get ready to start chanting in a minute.' He raised the megaphone again and began haranguing the folks below.

But then, as people began to recognise us and catch on to our intentions, there were signs of consternation and panic, especially among the gang's relatives.

'Are you crazy? Get down here this minute!' was the gist of the cries.

'No way!' boomed the megaphone. 'We're staying put until we get some definite promises that will bring this place back to life and make it worth living in. Our local MP has a surgery in Bansfield tonight. Somebody ring him and get him over here.'

The MP did drive up eventually, much to my surprise, but before he arrived there began the chanting of a great list of demands, followed by a chorus of WHAT DO

WE WANT? ALL OF THIS. WHEN DO WE WANT IT? – NOW!

The others had obviously rehearsed the list to perfection but I didn't know the words so I could only join in the chorus. It was just as well, for I needed to keep my mind on other things. I placed myself right next to Vern and was ready to leap into action if he made the slightest move. I hoped he wasn't going to, for I was terrified he might drag me with him. One glance over the edge of that crumbling parapet had turned my innards to jelly.

Down below, the crowd was growing more and more agitated. There was now lots of activity; running and jostling; lights going on; mobiles busy; bikes and a couple of cars turning up; even a farm tractor rolled onto the scene. Then somebody staggered along with a searchlight, snaked the cable off into the church, switched the thing on, directed it upwards and lit the whole tower.

'That's better!' Ben cried happily. 'And here comes the Press!'

As he spoke, a van drove up and two men

leapt out, one plunging into the crowd with a Dictaphone and the other directing a large and businesslike camera lens at ourselves. That was when the second lot of chanting started, after which Ben, with a great grin on his face, lit the first firework – a rocket he'd placed in a jam jar.

Meanwhile, the local constable, who had already shouted himself hoarse, had recruited helpers to batter at the door at the base of the tower which had been locked and strongly barricaded by Haz, the last one up. The banging and shouting lasted quite a while until the constable changed tactics and rang the fire brigade.

The minute Ben's rocket soared into the sky the kids below gave whoops of delight. This was the cue for more fireworks to follow, lending the whole affair a carnival atmosphere. Ben was in his element, cock-a-hoop with the success of his plan. He couldn't light the fireworks fast enough. Yet although he'd found a fairly sheltered corner for this, it was still too windy for safety. Sparks were blowing all over the place and I called to him to stop.

'Not likely! This is just what we need – a bit of colour and excitement! A night to remember.'

Headstrong and determined, that was Ben. Pig-headed, some might say; there was no arguing with him. But there was no arguing with the elements either; I suddenly smelled burning. The flapping banner had caught alight. A flaming shred of it tore free and blew backwards onto the roof, and in no time at all the ancient wooden decking had begun to smoulder. It had been a hot week and the boards were tinder dry. Even as I jumped forward, hoping to stamp out the problem, one end of the decking actually burst into flames and I had to retreat.

I yelled a warning. 'Back downstairs, quick!'

Ellie saw the danger and ran towards the trap door, dragging Katy with her. Haz started to follow, but Ben shouted for them to come back.

'Don't be such wimps! It's nothing – I'll have it out in a jiff.' He tore off his jacket and beat at the flames with it. 'You can't go now! You'll ruin everything.'

For a moment the three of them hesitated. Then Vern cried, 'Oh, let them go! You two as well. Clear off, the lot of you. I can manage this on my own.'

He swung round and pushed me away, taking me by surprise as I'd been focusing my attention on the fire. It was quite a vicious push. I lost my balance and fell backwards, and before I could struggle to my feet I saw Vern trying to stamp out the fire. He was jumping about all over the place and the bottoms of his jeans had caught alight. Suddenly he lurched sideways, staggered towards the very edge of the parapet and – with a terrifying cry – hurtled out into space.

9

Sunday, 22nd July

Spelswick's village police station – also about to be closed – was nothing more than the front parlour of one of Green Lane's terraced cottages. Last night, after the ambulance had taken Vern away and the fire crew had dealt with the flames, Harry Posner, the local constable, had ushered the remaining five of us into this parlour. But he'd soon realised that we were all too upset to talk coherently, so he gave us mugs of sweet tea and sent us home, ordering us to be back there at nine o'clock next morning.

So here we were, drifting in one by one, stunned by last night's dreadful outcome and expecting the worst. We all feared that

Vern was either dead or dying, but we daren't ask. None of us had the heart to speak. Feeling guilty and ashamed, we just sat where the constable placed us and awaited our punishment.

Harry Posner took a deep breath, but before he could speak Brenda Voysey walked in.

'Excuse me, Constable, but may I have a word with them first? I think you know what I'm going to tell them.'

Harry didn't look too pleased.

'Can't it wait?'

'No. I saw how upset Matthew was last night. They're all upset, but I think I can make them feel better.'

Harry shrugged. 'If you must. But make it snappy.'

Brenda turned to face us – and a pathetic bunch we were, slumped against the wall in varying stages of mental and physical collapse.

'Come on now, brace up! Things aren't so bad. As I'm sure the constable must have told you, your friend survived his accident. The fire crew broke his fall. He's dislocated a shoulder, broken an ankle and collected a few superficial burns and bruises but he'll live to tell the tale.'

She said 'accident'. And 'survived'! And no, Posner hadn't told us; the miserable rat was making us sweat.

The relief was tremendous. We could see one another coming back to life, sitting up in our chairs, lifting our faces like flowers to the sun. It didn't occur to us right then to wonder what Brenda had to do with all this. Our main concern was for Vern.

We all started asking questions. How long would he be in hospital? Could we go and see him? Had it landed him in trouble? How did his dad react? And so on.

Brenda waited patiently until all this had been sorted out, then she said: 'It's just a pity you lot didn't air your grievances in the proper manner and save a lot of trouble and worry. You must have seen me snooping around, watching you all, seeing your difficulties. And wanting to make things better.'

'Save your energy,' Haz told her. 'It won't

make any difference. You see where our efforts got us?'

'Ah, but I have a special motive. You are all too young to remember my mother, though some of your grandparents might. She used to love this village, especially your house, Matthew. She was always talking about it, especially the garden and that cherry tree she was so fond of. I'd never been here until last week; I'd only seen photographs, but even before I arrived I knew Spelswick was a place worth saving. And that's what I hope to do.'

What was the woman talking about?

We were all completely baffled.

It seemed Brenda's mother, Harriet Waldron – the woman in the photograph I'd found – had been wrongly convicted of the murder of the drowned girl Ellie had mentioned. Harriet had served a long prison sentence, at the beginning of which she had borne her daughter Perdita and the child had been whisked away into care. Harriet had eventually died in Walverton Women's Prison, so she never knew that with the advent of DNA her innocence was belatedly proved. The murdered girl's parents were the real culprits. Now Brenda, that prison-born 'lost' Perdita and her mother's heir, had been awarded a large amount of compensation.

'Which I aim to spend on Spelswick in my mother's memory. Every time I visited her she insisted that one day I should come back here to show that we had nothing to be ashamed of.'

'I couldn't believe my luck when I saw the advert for a lodger. It didn't take long to appreciate all your problems. So when I discovered that the White House was up for sale I bought it – for conversion into a Community Centre.

'The whole top floor can be yours; somewhere to meet and do whatever takes your fancy. There'll be money to fix it up the way you want it.'

There was silence while we took this in. Then, shamefaced, I said, 'We'd no idea! We never guessed you were on our side and willing to help.'

'Matt said you'd come from prison.'

Brenda actually smiled.

'In a way, I had. I became friends with the Warden and spent a few days with her before coming on here. She gave me a lift as far as the prison gates where the taxi picked me up.'

'Well, it's great, what you're doing,' said Ben cautiously, 'but it doesn't solve the real problems of this village. A Community Hall's fine, but wouldn't it have been better to spend the money on other things? Reopening the post office, for a start?'

Brenda smiled again; it was becoming a habit.

'Don't worry, that's taken care of, too. I intend to rescue the post office using a rota of paid volunteers which you lot can help me to recruit.'

'Wicked! While we're at it then, why don't we get up a petition for a bus service, even if it's only once a day?'

I thought that was a bit over the top, but this astonishing woman told us she'd already had words with the local MP and he'd promised to help.

'And if there's any money or energy left

after all that, we may even be able to do something about the primary school, though we can't make any promises.'

After a pause for breath she added:

'This was all supposed to be a big surprise, to be announced at a special village meeting I'd intended to call on August Bank Holiday Monday, but of course you impulsive lot have robbed me of my moment of glory.'

I, for one, began to feel thoroughly embarrassed and guilty.

'What can we say?' I muttered.

'Save your breath for making plans,' said Brenda, and smiled again.

Harry Posner had fidgeted all the way through this story and was obviously dying to intervene. This was his last chance to assert his authority here, since his office was about to close – it seemed not even Brenda could alter that – and he meant to make the most of it.

'You needn't think any of this lets you lot off the hook,' he told us. 'You behaved disgracefully and you deserve to be punished. You can thank your lucky stars – and a welltrained fire crew – that the whole blessed village didn't burn down. Sergeant Buckleby's on his way from Bansfield and he'll sort you out good and proper. All your parents will be coming along presently to hear what the Sergeant has to say.'

The gang all tried to look remorseful but it wasn't a great success. They were too buoyed up by their suddenly-glowing future prospects – and their lucky escape from the worst consequences of the past. As for me, I kept a very low profile. I'd already had thunderclaps of trouble from Mum, with threats of worse to follow.

'You tell your sergeant that what these young ones need is a good, long spell of Community Service,' suggested Brenda. 'Keep them occupied, it will do them a world of good. And I've got plenty of tasks lined up. The minute the Colonel moves out they can start work on the White House, and believe me, it won't be easy. Lots of alterations will have to be done. We'll need new plumbing for more toilets and a crèche, library shelving, a new spring floor for dancing, fresh decorations throughout – and that's just the start. There'll be proper workmen in charge, of course, but they're going to need a team of young, strong and willing unpaid labourers to keep the costs down. And there'll be no slacking. Vernon's father has agreed to act as full-time supervisor at the White House, so he'll keep them up to scratch. Then when they've finished that to everybody's satisfaction they can help me reorganise the shop. If they all work nine to five every day of the school holidays I expect we'll begin to see progress.'

I didn't mind that; it sounded tough, but fun. I knew my worst punishment would come from home. Mum has a very long memory and is slow to forgive, which was largely the cause of the split-up in the first place. I was destined never to live this down, but at least now there would be somewhere to escape to.

'How could you be so irresponsible?' Mum had cried last night. 'Surely we brought you up to have more sense than that? Goodness only knows what your father's going to say.'

She'd already summoned him home and

regarded the whole business, starting with the vicar's dinner, as a huge, wicked conspiracy. She felt she had been shabbily betrayed.

'I cannot believe that such a mad, stupid, dangerous idea could even be conceived, never mind put into action, and to think that my son . . . !' Etcetera, etcetera.

I tried to persuade her that there must be some part of this escapade she could use in her next novel, but she was not impressed.

10

Monday, 23rd July

On Monday morning Ellie was at our gate again, furiously ringing her bicycle bell before we had even put breakfast on the table.

'Oh, go and see what she wants, if only to shut her up,' Mum called tetchily from the kitchen. Obviously she hadn't forgiven Ellie either.

I saw immediately that Ellie was totally transformed from the miserable wretch of Friday to a glowing, enthusiastic sprite. She was wearing a fetching yellow top and white shorts, and had twirled her rusty locks into a sophisticated chignon. With all that hair out of the way, letting the light into her eyes and smile, her face seemed a good deal improved. In fact, she'd turned out to be not so bad-looking after all.

'Have you got any paint left over?' she demanded before I'd finished staring. It seemed she had already worked out a colour scheme for a games room in our allotted part of the Centre, and it included much 'serene green'.

'Don't you ever sleep?' I grumbled.

'Not when life's this good,' she replied happily. 'Sleep's a waste of time. Vern's doing great, he'll be home in a few days – and IT WAS JUST AN ACCIDENT.' She emphasised that last bit with evident relief.

'I know.'

'Besides, he'll be able to stay on at school now his dad's got a job. Ben's happy because we're going to get the village improvements he's worked so hard for – and for which he'll claim most of the credit, like as not. And Katy and Haz are happy because they've made up and got back together again.'

'Oh! – I thought you and Haz...'

Ellie laughed. 'Me and spotty Harold? You must be joking! I was just obligingly helping him to make Katy jealous, and it worked. Well, I usually get my own way in the end.'

I stood and stared with my mouth half-open. 'Oh!' I said again. How idiotic was that?

'Well, come on, let's go and fetch this paint,' Ellie cried, grabbing hold of me and whirling me joyously over Brenda's newly-manicured lawn.

'My dad's just rung,' I said when I could breathe again. 'He's coming home tomorrow. So I'll be going up to Manchester for a mini break before we have to start this community service.'

I was dreading his wrath so it didn't seem such a tempting prospect after all, despite the chance of a break from Mum...until Ellie cried, 'Wow! Can I come, too? I'm dying to see Manchester and this famous flat of yours. Besides, you've already invited me once, remember? You can't go back on it now.'

I stared, blushed, stared some more, then said, 'Oh, do you really want to come?'

'Thought you'd never ask. It's just what we need, you and me, to give us time to get to know each other a bit better – without your mum and Brenda breathing down our necks, not to mention the rest of the gang. I reckon we got off on the wrong foot last week, don't you?'

'Yeah, I guess I was too busy trying to lay a non-existent ghost,' I said, suddenly certain that our house wasn't haunted after all.

About the Author

I was brought up in North Lancashire in the lovely Pendle Valley and spent most of my primary school playtimes inventing games which consited largely of a lot of running around and screaming. At age 9 a first poem was published in the local paper and a one-act play performed in school. This lasted all of ten minutes. In the holidays my friends and I used to explore the countryside with a picnic, telling one another stories on the way – and never an adult in sight! Such a shame that today's children don't have this kind of freedom. At university I worked on the student newspaper, writing humorous verse to fill gaps left by advertisers who let us down. Then someone suggested I write a bit of verse for *PUNCH*, so I did, and they not only published it but paid what I thought of as a small fortune! So I kept on sending more, and they kept on publishing them. Then the assistant editor steered me onto writing prose. One week a box of children's books arrived to be reviewed for a special feature, and I was hooked! I enjoyed them so much I thought I might like to have a go at writing one some day. After university there followed a crash course in shorthand and typing, which is the most useful thing I ever learnt, and a course in librarianship. This led to a post as Young People's Services librarian, which meant coming into contact with many more children's books and authors. I began to notice that there was a gap in the market for the very short, fast-moving book to cater for less willing readers. The first book was published in 1975 since when another 69 have followed. I visit schools quite frequently to help children with their creative writing and to hope they will help me with mine. I had a really happy marriage but am now widowed. I have a son and daughter, and four grandchildren. The most popular book seems to be *The Speckled Panic*, which has been in print almost continuously since 1982. But my own favourites are the Deathwood stories: *The Deathwood Letters* and *Dark Deeds at Deathwood*. A third one, *Deathwood Damian Strikes Again*, will follow shortly. I love writing, especially children's books. It's the best job in the world.

The Deathwood Letters
Hazel Townson

Damian Drake rescues his dog from a well and
gets his name into the newspapers.
He then receives a letter from a girl he
has never met which sparks off a long
correspondence between the two. As more and
more letters are exchanged a sinister thread
creeps in and the story gathers speed for a final
amazing drama.

'A very cleverly constructed thriller'
Books for Keeps

ISBN 978 1 84270 228 4

The Invisible Boy
Hazel Townson
Illustrated by Tony Ross

Gary suspects he is turning invisible and blames the
door-key he has to wear round his neck. Could it
be a magic key? He decides to hide so that people
will have to search and find him, thus proving that
he isn't invisible after all. But first there are one
or two problems in the way, such as a mysterious
box of chocolates, a bloodstained body in an
amusement arcade, a space-ship and an alien
on the headland, all of which turn Gary's
flight into a nightmare.

ISBN 978 1 84270 1058

Two Weird Weeks
Hazel Townson

Sonia Johnson's diary charts her two-week
infatuation with the enigmatic Owen Gates. In
alternate chapters Owen's diary reveals his
heartless determination to exploit Sonia's good
nature for his own unsavoury purposes as he
searches for the buried proceeds of a robbery.

'It's very fast paced . . . skilful,
uncontrived and humorous.'
Manchester Evening News

ISBN 978 1 84270 0730

Disaster Bag
Hazel Townson
Illustrated by David McKee

Colin Laird is seriously worried about the state of
the world. Disasters are happening all round him,
and he decides to acquire a Disaster Bag filled with
all the equipment he might need in an emergency.
Only then does he begin to feel safe. But how
could he possibly guess that a terrorist would slip a
bomb into his bag when he wasn't looking...?

'One of Townson's best'
Books for Keeps

ISBN 978 0 86264 524 3